CW00868141

Ruby and Kylie's Fairy Time

ORCHARD BOOKS
338 Euston Road, London NW1 3BH
Orchard Books Australia
Level 17/207 Kent Street, Sydney, NSW 2000

First published in 2009 by Orchard Books.

© 2009 Rainbow Magic Limited.
A HIT Entertainment company. Rainbow Magic
is a trademark of Rainbow Magic Limited.
Reg. U.S. Pat. & Tm. Off. And other countries.

All fairy illustrations © Georgie Ripper 2009.
All other illustrations © Orchard Books 2009 based
on underlying copyright owned by Georgie Ripper.

A CIP catalogue record for this book is available
from the British Library.

ISBN 978 1 40830 552 2

1 3 5 7 9 10 8 6 4 2

Printed in Italy by Rotolito Lombarda
Orchard Books is a division of Hachette Children's Books,
an Hachette UK company
www.hachette.co.uk

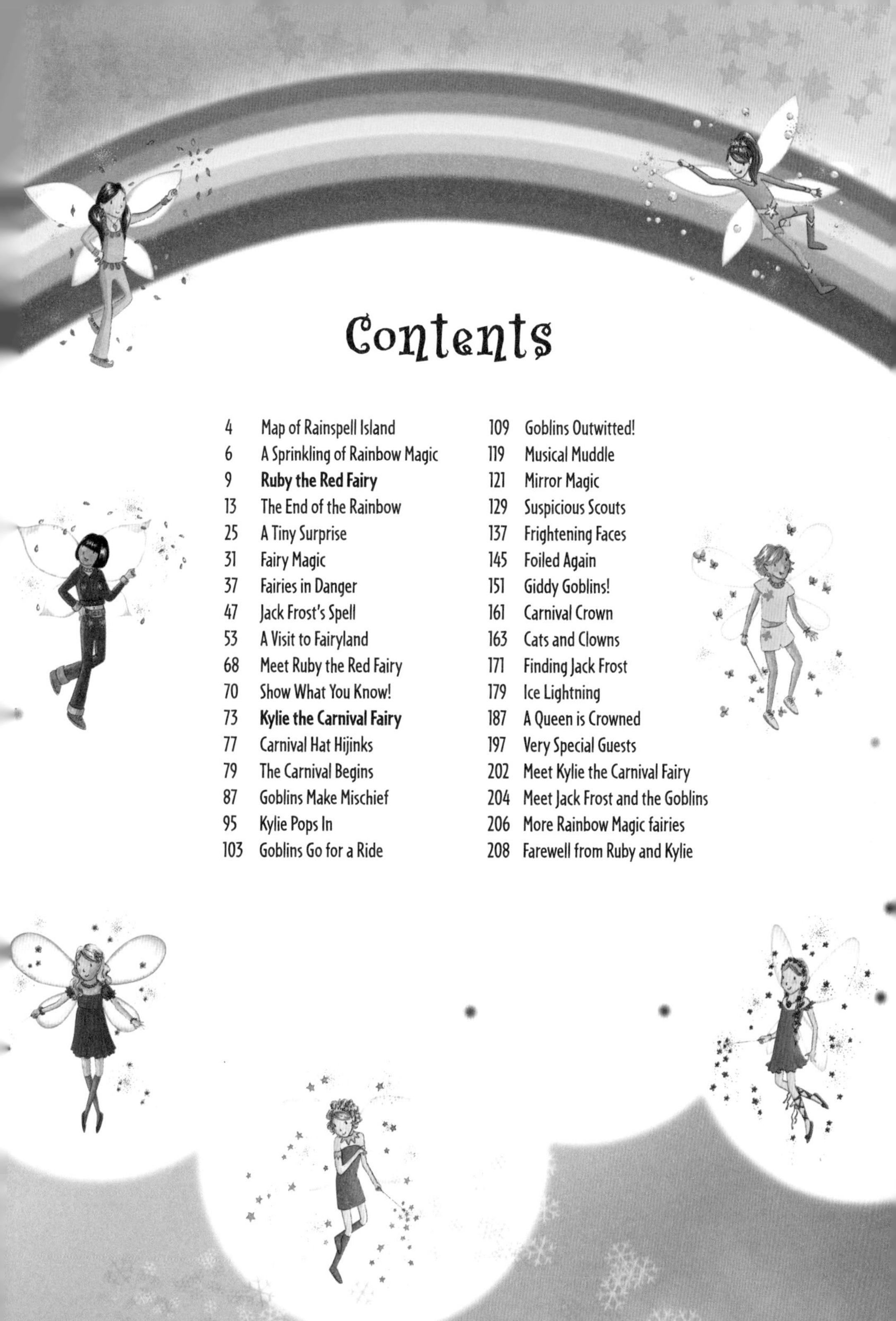

Contents

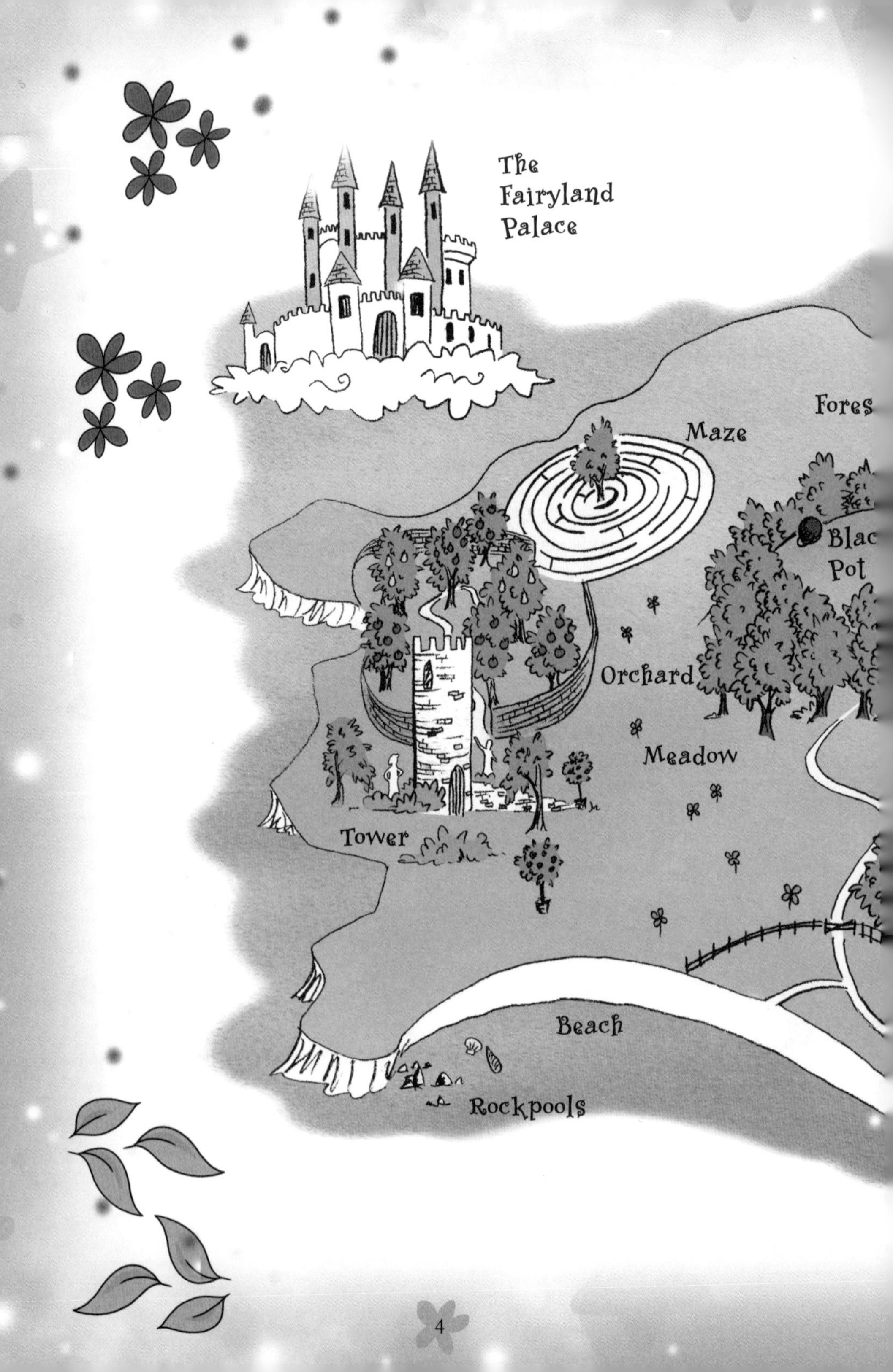
The
Fairyland
Palace
Maze
Fores
Blac
Pot
Orchard
Meadow
Tower
Beach
Rockpools

Rainspell Island
Jack
Frost's
Ice Castle
Willow
Tree
Stream
Field
Town
ermaid
ottage
Harbour
Dolphin
Cottage

A Sprinkling Of Rainbow Magic

In this book you will read all about Ruby the Red Fairy. Here she is with her six rainbow sisters!

The seven
Rainbow Fairies
have each cast a special
friendship spell for you.
Try reading them out
to your best friend!

Ruby the Red Fairy

My spell is for smiles
and a thousand kind acts.
Making a friend
is a wonderful pact!

Write down some of the nicest things your best friend has ever done for you and the things you like most about them.

Amber the Orange Fairy

My spell is for parties
and meeting to play!
Chatting with friends
will brighten your day.

Saffron the Yellow Fairy

My spell is for being there
no matter what.
A friend you can count on
is worth such a lot!

Good times and bad...

When Jack Frost didn't get invited to the Midsummer Ball, he caused so much trouble! The ice lord took the colours away from Fairyland by banishing the Rainbow Fairies to the human world. Thank goodness Kirsty and Rachel were there to help them – true friends in times of need!

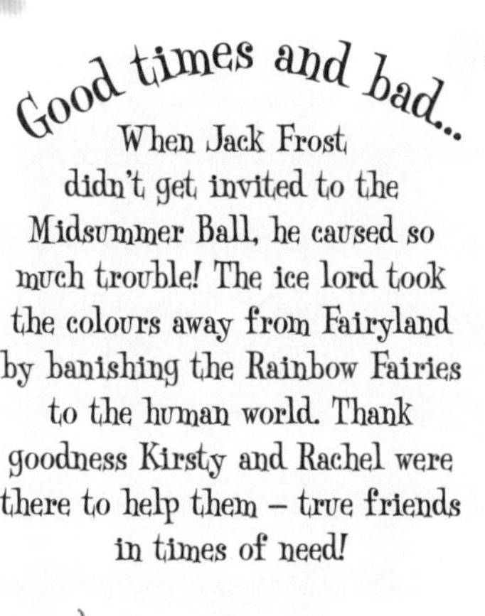

Heather the Violet Fairy

My spell is for help,
splitting problems in two.
You never know when your
friend may need you!

Izzy the Indigo Fairy

My spell is for giggles,
for laughs in the sun.
Friendship is priceless,
but most of all fun!

Sky the Blue Fairy

My spell is for whispers
and secrets to share.
Open your heart
to someone who'll care!

Fern the Green Fairy

My spell is for trying
out daring new things.
Do them together –
you'll be lifted on wings!

Ruby the Red Fairy

Cold winds blow and thick ice form –
I conjure up this fairy storm.
To seven corners of the mortal world
the Rainbow Fairies will be hurled!

I curse every part of Fairyland,
with a frosty wave of my icy hand.
For now and always, from this fateful day,
Fairyland will be cold and grey!

Ruby's Story

Read on to find out what happened to Ruby and her rainbow sisters when they forgot to invite a very important person to the Midsummer Ball!

Contents

The End of the Rainbow

"Look, Dad!" said Rachel Walker. She pointed across the blue-green sea at the rocky island ahead of them. The ferry was sailing towards it, dipping up and down on the rolling waves. "Is that Rainspell Island?" she asked.

Her dad nodded. "Yes, it is," he said, smiling. "Our holiday is about to begin!"

The waves slapped against the side of the ferry as it bobbed up and down on the water. Rachel felt her heart thump with excitement. She could see white cliffs and emerald green fields on the island. And golden sandy beaches, with rock pools dotted here and there.

Suddenly, a few fat raindrops plopped down onto Rachel's head. "Oh!" she gasped, surprised. The sun was still shining.

Rachel's mum grabbed her hand.

"Let's get under cover," she said, leading Rachel inside.

"Isn't that strange?" Rachel said. "Sunshine *and* rain!"

"Let's hope the rain stops before we get off the ferry," said Mr Walker. "Now, where did I put that map of the island?"

Rachel looked out of the window. Her eyes opened wide.

A girl was standing alone on the deck. Her dark hair was wet with raindrops, but she didn't seem to care. She just stared up at the sky.

Rachel looked over at her mum and dad. They were busy studying the map. So Rachel slipped back outside to see what was so interesting.

And there it was. In the blue sky, high above them, was the most amazing rainbow that Rachel had ever seen. One end of the rainbow was far out to sea. The other seemed to fall somewhere on Rainspell Island. All of the colours were bright and clear.

"Isn't it perfect?" the dark-haired girl whispered to Rachel.

"Yes, it is," Rachel agreed. "Are you going to Rainspell on holiday?"

The girl nodded. "We're staying for a week," she said. "I'm Kirsty Tate."

Rachel smiled, as the rain began to stop. "I'm Rachel Walker. We're staying at Mermaid Cottage," she added.

"And we're at Dolphin Cottage," said Kirsty. "Do you think we might be near each other?"

"I hope so," Rachel replied. She had a feeling she was going to like Kirsty.

Kirsty leaned over the rail and looked down into the shimmering water. "The sea looks really deep, doesn't it?" she said. "There might even be mermaids down there, watching us right now!"

Rachel stared at the waves. She saw something that made her heart skip a beat.

"Look!" she said. "Is that a mermaid's hair?" Then she laughed, when she saw that it was just seaweed.

"It could be a mermaid's necklace," said Kirsty, smiling. "Maybe she lost it when she was trying to escape from a sea monster."

The ferry was now sailing into Rainspell's tiny harbour. Seagulls flew around them, and fishing boats bobbed on the water.

"Look at that big cliff over there," Kirsty said. She pointed it out to Rachel. "It looks a bit like a giant's face, doesn't it?"

Rachel looked, and nodded. Kirsty seemed to see magic *everywhere*.

"There you are, Rachel!" called Mrs Walker. Rachel turned round and saw her mum and dad coming out onto the deck.

"We'll be getting off the ferry in a few minutes," Mrs Walker added.

"Mum, Dad, this is Kirsty," Rachel said. "She's staying at Dolphin Cottage."

"That's right next door to ours," said Mr Walker. "I remember seeing it on the map."

Rachel and Kirsty looked at each other in delight.

"I'd better go and find *my* mum and dad," said Kirsty. She looked round. "Here they are."

Kirsty's mum and dad came over to say hello to the Walkers. Then the ferry docked, and everyone began to leave the boat.

"Our cottages are on the other side of the harbour," said Rachel's dad, looking at the map. "It's not far."

Mermaid Cottage and Dolphin Cottage were right next to the beach. Rachel loved her bedroom, which was high up, in the attic. From the window, she could see the waves rolling onto the sand.

A shout from outside made her look down. It was Kirsty. She was standing under the window, waving at her.

"Let's go and explore the beach!" Kirsty called.

Rachel dashed outside to join her.

Seaweed lay in piles on the sand, and there were tiny pink and white shells dotted about.

"I love it here already!" Rachel shouted happily above the noise of the seagulls.

"Me too," Kirsty said. She pointed up at the sky. "Look, the rainbow's still there."

Rachel looked up. The rainbow glowed brightly among the fluffy white clouds.

"Have you heard the story about a pot of gold at the end of the rainbow?" Kirsty asked.

Rachel nodded. "Yes, but that's just in fairy stories," she said.

Kirsty grinned. "Maybe. But let's go and find out for ourselves!"

"OK," Rachel agreed. "We can explore the island at the same time."

They rushed back to tell their parents where they were going. Then Kirsty and Rachel set off along a lane behind the cottages. It led them away from the beach, across green fields, and towards a small wood.

Rachel kept looking up at the rainbow. She was worried that it would start to fade now that the rain had stopped. But the colours stayed clear and bright.

"It looks like the end of the rainbow is over there," Kirsty said. "Come on!"

And she hurried towards the trees.

The wood was cool and green after the heat of the sun. Rachel and Kirsty followed a winding path until they came to a clearing. Then they both stopped and stared.

The rainbow shone down onto the grass through a gap in the trees.

And there, at the rainbow's end, lay an old, black pot.

A Tiny Surprise

"Look!" Kirsty whispered. "There really is a pot of gold!"

"It could just be a cooking pot," Rachel said doubtfully. "Some campers might have left it behind."

But Kirsty shook her head. "I don't think so," she said. "It looks really old."

Rachel stared at the pot. It was sitting on the grass, upside down.

"Let's have a closer look," said Kirsty. She ran to the pot and tried to turn it over. "Oh, it's heavy!" she gasped. She tried again, but the pot didn't move.

Rachel rushed to help her. They both pushed and pushed at the pot. This time it moved, just a little.

"Let's try again," Kirsty panted. "Are you ready, Rachel?"

Tap! Tap! Tap!

Rachel and Kirsty stared at each other.

"What was that?" Rachel gasped.

"I don't know," whispered Kirsty.

Tap! Tap!

"There it is again," Kirsty said. She looked down at the pot lying on the grass. "You know what? I think it's coming from inside this pot!"

Rachel's eyes opened wide. "Are you sure?" She bent down, and put her ear to the pot. *Tap! Tap!* Then, to her amazement, Rachel heard a tiny voice.

"Help!" it called. "Help me!"

Rachel grabbed Kirsty's arm. "Did you hear that?" she asked.

Kirsty nodded. "Quick!" she said. "We *must* turn the pot over!"

Rachel and Kirsty pushed at the pot as hard as they could. It began to rock from side to side on the grass.

"We're nearly there!" Rachel panted. "Keep pushing, Kirsty!"

The girls pushed with all their might.

Suddenly, the pot turned over and rolled onto its side. Rachel and Kirsty were taken by surprise. They both lost their balance and landed on the grass with a thump.

"Look!" Kirsty whispered, breathing hard.

A small shower of sparkling red dust had flown out of the pot. Rachel and Kirsty gasped with surprise. The dust hung in the air above them. And there, right in the middle of the glittering cloud, was a tiny winged girl.

Rachel and Kirsty watched in wonder as the

CW00868141

Ruby and Kylie's Fairy Time

ORCHARD BOOKS
338 Euston Road, London NW1 3BH
Orchard Books Australia
Level 17/207 Kent Street, Sydney, NSW 2000

First published in 2009 by Orchard Books.

© 2009 Rainbow Magic Limited.
A HIT Entertainment company. Rainbow Magic
is a trademark of Rainbow Magic Limited.
Reg. U.S. Pat. & Tm. Off. And other countries.

All fairy illustrations © Georgie Ripper 2009.
All other illustrations © Orchard Books 2009 based
on underlying copyright owned by Georgie Ripper.

A CIP catalogue record for this book is available
from the British Library.

ISBN 978 1 40830 552 2

1 3 5 7 9 10 8 6 4 2

Printed in Italy by Rotolito Lombarda
Orchard Books is a division of Hachette Children's Books,
an Hachette UK company
www.hachette.co.uk

Contents

The Fairyland Palace
Maze
Fores
Blac
Pot
Orchard
Meadow
Tower
Beach
Rockpools

Rainspell Island
Jack Frost's Ice Castle
Willow Tree
Stream
Field
Town
ermaid
ottage
Harbour
Dolphin Cottage

A Sprinkling of Rainbow Magic

In this book you will read all about Ruby the Red Fairy. Here she is with her six rainbow sisters!

The seven Rainbow Fairies have each cast a special friendship spell for you. Try reading them out to your best friend!

Ruby the Red Fairy

My spell is for smiles
and a thousand kind acts.
Making a friend
is a wonderful pact!

Write down some of the nicest things your best friend has ever done for you and the things you like most about them.

Amber the Orange Fairy

My spell is for parties
and meeting to play!
Chatting with friends
will brighten your day.

Saffron the Yellow Fairy

My spell is for being there
no matter what.
A friend you can count on
is worth such a lot!

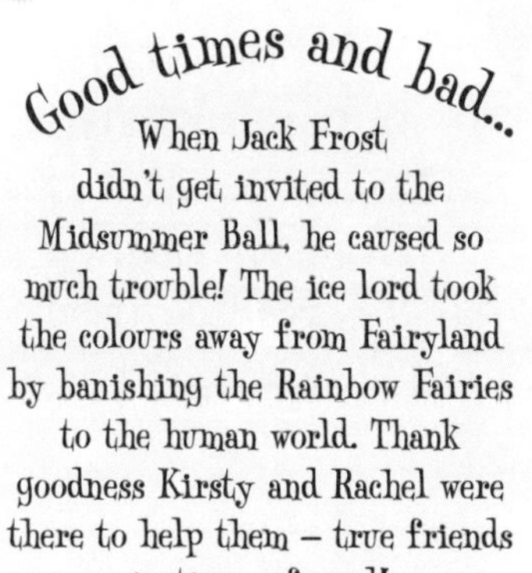

Good times and bad...

When Jack Frost didn't get invited to the Midsummer Ball, he caused so much trouble! The ice lord took the colours away from Fairyland by banishing the Rainbow Fairies to the human world. Thank goodness Kirsty and Rachel were there to help them – true friends in times of need!

Heather the Violet Fairy

My spell is for help,
splitting problems in two.
You never know when your
friend may need you!

Izzy the Indigo Fairy

My spell is for giggles,
for laughs in the sun.
Friendship is priceless,
but most of all fun!

Sky the Blue Fairy

My spell is for whispers
and secrets to share.
Open your heart
to someone who'll care!

Fern the Green Fairy

My spell is for trying
out daring new things.
Do them together –
you'll be lifted on wings!

Ruby the Red Fairy

Cold winds blow and thick ice form –
I conjure up this fairy storm.
To seven corners of the mortal world
the Rainbow Fairies will be hurled!

I curse every part of Fairyland,
with a frosty wave of my icy hand.
For now and always, from this fateful day,
Fairyland will be cold and grey!

Read on to find out what happened to Ruby and her rainbow sisters when they forgot to invite a very important person to the Midsummer Ball!

Contents

The End of the Rainbow

"Look, Dad!" said Rachel Walker. She pointed across the blue-green sea at the rocky island ahead of them. The ferry was sailing towards it, dipping up and down on the rolling waves. "Is that Rainspell Island?" she asked.

Her dad nodded. "Yes, it is," he said, smiling. "Our holiday is about to begin!"

The waves slapped against the side of the ferry as it bobbed up and down on the water. Rachel felt her heart thump with excitement. She could see white cliffs and emerald green fields on the island. And golden sandy beaches, with rock pools dotted here and there.

Suddenly, a few fat raindrops plopped down onto Rachel's head. "Oh!" she gasped, surprised. The sun was still shining.

Rachel's mum grabbed her hand.

"Let's get under cover," she said, leading Rachel inside.

"Isn't that strange?" Rachel said. "Sunshine *and* rain!"

"Let's hope the rain stops before we get off the ferry," said Mr Walker. "Now, where did I put that map of the island?"

Rachel looked out of the window. Her eyes opened wide.

A girl was standing alone on the deck. Her dark hair was wet with raindrops, but she didn't seem to care. She just stared up at the sky.

Rachel looked over at her mum and dad. They were busy studying the map. So Rachel slipped back outside to see what was so interesting.

And there it was. In the blue sky, high above them, was the most amazing rainbow that Rachel had ever seen. One end of the rainbow was far out to sea. The other seemed to fall somewhere on Rainspell Island. All of the colours were bright and clear.

"Isn't it perfect?" the dark-haired girl whispered to Rachel.

"Yes, it is," Rachel agreed. "Are you going to Rainspell on holiday?"

The girl nodded. "We're staying for a week," she said. "I'm Kirsty Tate."

Rachel smiled, as the rain began to stop. "I'm Rachel Walker. We're staying at Mermaid Cottage," she added.

"And we're at Dolphin Cottage," said Kirsty. "Do you think we might be near each other?"

"I hope so," Rachel replied. She had a feeling she was going to like Kirsty.

Kirsty leaned over the rail and looked down into the shimmering water. "The sea looks really deep, doesn't it?" she said. "There might even be mermaids down there, watching us right now!"

Rachel stared at the waves. She saw something that made her heart skip a beat.

"Look!" she said. "Is that a mermaid's hair?" Then she laughed, when she saw that it was just seaweed.

"It could be a mermaid's necklace," said Kirsty, smiling. "Maybe she lost it when she was trying to escape from a sea monster."

The ferry was now sailing into Rainspell's tiny harbour. Seagulls flew around them, and fishing boats bobbed on the water.

"Look at that big cliff over there," Kirsty said. She pointed it out to Rachel. "It looks a bit like a giant's face, doesn't it?"

Rachel looked, and nodded. Kirsty seemed to see magic *everywhere*.

"There you are, Rachel!" called Mrs Walker. Rachel turned round and saw her mum and dad coming out onto the deck.

"We'll be getting off the ferry in a few minutes," Mrs Walker added.

"Mum, Dad, this is Kirsty," Rachel said. "She's staying at Dolphin Cottage."

"That's right next door to ours," said Mr Walker. "I remember seeing it on the map."

Rachel and Kirsty looked at each other in delight.

"I'd better go and find *my* mum and dad," said Kirsty. She looked round. "Here they are."

Kirsty's mum and dad came over to say hello to the Walkers. Then the ferry docked, and everyone began to leave the boat.

"Our cottages are on the other side of the harbour," said Rachel's dad, looking at the map. "It's not far."

Mermaid Cottage and Dolphin Cottage were right next to the beach. Rachel loved her bedroom, which was high up, in the attic. From the window, she could see the waves rolling onto the sand.

A shout from outside made her look down. It was Kirsty. She was standing under the window, waving at her.

"Let's go and explore the beach!" Kirsty called.

Rachel dashed outside to join her.

Seaweed lay in piles on the sand, and there were tiny pink and white shells dotted about.

"I love it here already!" Rachel shouted happily above the noise of the seagulls.

"Me too," Kirsty said. She pointed up at the sky. "Look, the rainbow's still there."

Rachel looked up. The rainbow glowed brightly among the fluffy white clouds.

"Have you heard the story about a pot of gold at the end of the rainbow?" Kirsty asked.

Rachel nodded. "Yes, but that's just in fairy stories," she said.

Kirsty grinned. "Maybe. But let's go and find out for ourselves!"

"OK," Rachel agreed. "We can explore the island at the same time."

They rushed back to tell their parents where they were going. Then Kirsty and Rachel set off along a lane behind the cottages. It led them away from the beach, across green fields, and towards a small wood.

Rachel kept looking up at the rainbow. She was worried that it would start to fade now that the rain had stopped. But the colours stayed clear and bright.

"It looks like the end of the rainbow is over there," Kirsty said. "Come on!"

And she hurried towards the trees.

The wood was cool and green after the heat of the sun. Rachel and Kirsty followed a winding path until they came to a clearing. Then they both stopped and stared.

The rainbow shone down onto the grass through a gap in the trees.

And there, at the rainbow's end, lay an old, black pot.

"Look!" Kirsty whispered. "There really is a pot of gold!"

"It could just be a cooking pot," Rachel said doubtfully. "Some campers might have left it behind."

But Kirsty shook her head. "I don't think so," she said. "It looks really old."

Rachel stared at the pot. It was sitting on the grass, upside down.

"Let's have a closer look," said Kirsty. She ran to the pot and tried to turn it over. "Oh, it's heavy!" she gasped. She tried again, but the pot didn't move.

Rachel rushed to help her. They both pushed and pushed at the pot. This time it moved, just a little.

"Let's try again," Kirsty panted. "Are you ready, Rachel?"

Tap! Tap! Tap!

Rachel and Kirsty stared at each other.

"What was that?" Rachel gasped.

"I don't know," whispered Kirsty.

Tap! Tap!

"There it is again," Kirsty said. She looked down at the pot lying on the grass. "You know what? I think it's coming from inside this pot!"

Rachel's eyes opened wide. "Are you sure?" She bent down, and put her ear to the pot. *Tap! Tap!* Then, to her amazement, Rachel heard a tiny voice.

"Help!" it called. "Help me!"

Rachel grabbed Kirsty's arm. "Did you hear that?" she asked.

Kirsty nodded. "Quick!" she said. "We *must* turn the pot over!"

Rachel and Kirsty pushed at the pot as hard as they could. It began to rock from side to side on the grass.

"We're nearly there!" Rachel panted. "Keep pushing, Kirsty!"

The girls pushed with all their might.

Suddenly, the pot turned over and rolled onto its side. Rachel and Kirsty were taken by surprise. They both lost their balance and landed on the grass with a thump.

"Look!" Kirsty whispered, breathing hard.

A small shower of sparkling red dust had flown out of the pot. Rachel and Kirsty gasped with surprise. The dust hung in the air above them. And there, right in the middle of the glittering cloud, was a tiny winged girl.

Rachel and Kirsty watched in wonder as the

tiny girl fluttered in the sunlight, her delicate wings sparkling with all the colours of the rainbow.

"Oh, Rachel!" Kirsty whispered. "It's a fairy..."

Fairy Magic

The fairy flew over Rachel and Kirsty's heads. Her short, silky dress was the colour of ripe strawberries. Red crystal earrings glowed in her ears. Her golden hair was plaited with tiny red roses, and her little feet wore crimson slippers.

She waved her scarlet wand, and the shower of sparkling red fairy dust floated softly down to the ground. Where it landed, all sorts of red flowers appeared with a *pop!*

Rachel and Kirsty watched open-mouthed. It really and truly *was* a fairy.

"This is like a dream," Rachel said.

"I always believed in fairies," Kirsty whispered back. "But I never thought I'd ever *see* one!"

The fairy flew towards them. "Oh, thank you *so* much!" she called in a tiny, silvery voice. "I'm free at last!" She glided down, and landed on Kirsty's hand.

Kirsty gasped. The fairy felt lighter and softer than a butterfly.

"I was beginning to think I'd *never* get out of that pot!" the fairy said.

Kirsty wanted to ask the fairy so many things. But she didn't know where to start.

"Tell me your names, quickly," said the fairy. She fluttered up into the air again. "There's so much to be done, and we must get started right away."

Rachel wondered what the fairy meant. "I'm Rachel," she said.

"And I'm Kirsty," said Kirsty. "But who are *you?*"

"I'm the Red Rainbow Fairy – but call me Ruby," the fairy replied.

"Ruby..." Kirsty breathed. "A Rainbow Fairy..." She and Rachel stared at each other in excitement. This really *was* magic!

"Yes," said Ruby. "And I have six sisters: Amber, Saffron, Fern, Sky, Izzy and Heather. One for each colour of the rainbow, you see."

"What do Rainbow Fairies do?" Rachel asked.

Ruby flew over and landed lightly on Rachel's hand. "It's our job to put all the different colours into Fairyland," she explained.

"So why were you shut up inside that old pot?" asked Rachel.

"And where are your sisters?" Kirsty added.

Ruby's golden wings drooped. Her eyes filled with tiny, sparkling tears.

"I don't know," she said. "Something terrible has happened in Fairyland. We *really* need your help!"

Kirsty stared down at Ruby, sitting sadly on Rachel's hand. "Of course we'll help you!" she said.

"Just tell us how," added Rachel.

Ruby wiped the tears from her eyes. "Thank you!" she said. "But first I must show you the terrible thing that has happened. Follow me – as quickly as you can!" She flew into the air, her wings shimmering in the sunshine.

Rachel and Kirsty followed Ruby across the clearing. She danced ahead of them, glowing like a crimson flame. She stopped at a small pond under a weeping willow tree. "Look! I can show you what happened yesterday," she said.

She flew over the pond and scattered another shower of sparkling fairy dust with her tiny red wand. At once, the water lit up with a strange, silver light. It bubbled and fizzed, and then became still.

With wide eyes, Rachel and Kirsty watched as a picture appeared.

It was like looking through a window into another land!

"Oh, Rachel, look!" said Kirsty.

A river of brightest blue ran swiftly past hills of greenest green. Scattered on the hillsides were red and white toadstool houses. And on top of the highest hill stood a silver palace with four pink towers.

The towers were so high, their points were almost hidden by the fluffy white clouds floating past.

Hundreds of fairies were making their way towards the palace. Some were walking and some were flying. Rachel and Kirsty could see goblins, elves, imps and pixies, too. Everyone seemed very excited.

"Yesterday was the day of the Fairyland Midsummer Ball," Ruby explained. She flew over the pond and pointed down with her wand to a spot in the middle of the scene.

"There I am, with my rainbow sisters."

Kirsty and Rachel looked closely at where Ruby was pointing. They saw seven fairies, each dressed prettily in their own rainbow colour. Wherever they flew, they left a trail of fairy dust behind them.

"The Midsummer Ball is *very* special," Ruby went on. "And my sisters and I are always in charge of sending out invitations."

To the sound of tinkling music, the front doors of the palace slowly opened.

"Here come King Oberon and Queen Titania," said Ruby. "The Fairy King and Queen. They are about to begin the ball."

Kirsty and Rachel watched as the King and Queen stepped out. The King wore a splendid golden coat and a golden crown. His Queen wore a silver dress and a tiara that sparkledwith diamonds. Everyone cheered loudly. After a while, the King signalled for quiet. "Fairies," he began. "We are very glad to see you all here. Welcome to the Midsummer Ball!"

The fairies clapped their hands and cheered again. A band of green frogs in smart orange outfits started to play, and the dancing began.

Suddenly, a grey mist seemed to fill the room. Kirsty and Rachel watched in alarm as all the fairies started to shiver. And a loud, chilly voice shouted out, "Stop the music!"

The band fell silent. Everyone looked scared. A tall, bony figure was pushing his way through the crowd. He was dressed all in white, and there was frost on his white hair and beard. Icicles hung from his clothes. But his face was red and angry.

"Who's that?" Rachel asked with a shiver. Ice had begun to form around the edge of the pond.

"It's Jack Frost," said Ruby. And she shivered as well.

Jack Frost glared at the seven Rainbow Fairies. "Why wasn't I invited to the Midsummer Ball?" he asked coldly.

The Rainbow Fairies gasped in horror...

Ruby looked up from the pond picture. She smiled sadly at Rachel and Kirsty. "Yes, we forgot to invite Jack Frost," she said.

The Fairy Queen stepped forward. "You are very welcome, Jack Frost," she said. "Please stay and enjoy the ball."

But Jack Frost looked even more angry. "Too late!" he hissed. "You forgot to invite me!" He turned and pointed a thin, icy finger at the Rainbow Fairies.

"Well, you will not forget this!" he went on. "My spell will banish the Rainbow Fairies to the seven corners of the mortal world. From this day on, Fairyland will be without colour – for ever!"

As Jack Frost cast his spell, a great, icy wind began to blow. It picked up the seven Rainbow Fairies and spun them up into the darkening sky. The other fairies watched in dismay.

Jack Frost turned to the King and Queen. "Your Rainbow Fairies will be trapped, never to return." With that, he left, leaving a trail of icy footprints.

Quickly, the Fairy Queen stepped forward and lifted her silver wand.

"I cannot undo Jack Frost's magic completely," she shouted, as the wind howled and rushed around her. "But I can guide the Rainbow Fairies to a safe place until they can be rescued!"

The Queen pointed her wand at the grey sky overhead. A black pot came spinning through the stormy clouds. It flew towards the Rainbow Fairies. One by one, the Rainbow Fairies tumbled into the pot.

"Pot at the end of the rainbow, keep our Rainbow Fairies safely together," the Queen called. "And take them to Rainspell Island!"

The pot flew out of sight, behind a dark cloud. And the bright colours of Fairyland began to fade, until it looked like an old black and white photograph.

"Oh no!" Kirsty gasped. Then the picture in the pond vanished.

"So the Fairy Queen cast her *own* spell!" Rachel said. She was bursting with questions. "She put you and your sisters in the pot, and sent you to Rainspell."

Ruby nodded. "Our Queen knew that we would be safe here," she said. "We know Rainspell well. It is a place full of magic."

"But where are your sisters?" Kirsty wanted to know. "They were in the pot, too."

Ruby looked upset. "Jack Frost's spell must have been stronger than the Queen thought," she said. "As the pot spun through the sky, the wind blew my sisters out again. I was at the bottom, so I was safe. But I was trapped when the pot landed upside down."

"So are your sisters somewhere on Rainspell?" Kirsty asked.

Ruby nodded. "Yes, but they're scattered all over the island. Jack Frost's spell has trapped them as well." She flew towards Kirsty and landed on her shoulder. "That's where you and Rachel come in."

"How?" Rachel asked.

"You found *me* didn't you?" the fairy went on. "That's because you believe in magic." She flew from Kirsty's shoulder to Rachel's. "So, you could rescue my Rainbow sisters too! Then we can all bring colour back to Fairyland again."

A Visit to Fairyland

"Of course we'll search for your sisters," Kirsty said quickly. "Won't we, Rachel?"

Rachel nodded.

"Oh, thank you," Ruby said happily.

"But we're only here for a week," Rachel said. "Will that be long enough?"

"We must get started right away," said Ruby. "First, I must take you to Fairyland to meet our King and Queen. They will be very pleased to know that you are going to help me find my sisters."

Rachel and Kirsty stared at Ruby.

"You're taking us to *Fairyland*!" Kirsty gasped. She could hardly believe her ears. Nor could Rachel.

"But how will we get there?" Rachel wanted to know.

"We'll fly there," Ruby replied.

"But *we* can't fly!" Rachel pointed out.

Ruby smiled. She whirled up into the air and flew over the girls' heads. Then she swirled her wand above them. Magic red fairy dust fluttered down.

Rachel and Kirsty began to feel a bit strange. Were the trees getting bigger or were they getting smaller? *They were getting smaller!*

Smaller and smaller and smaller, until they were the same size as Ruby.

"I'm tiny!" Rachel laughed. She was so small, the flowers around her seemed like trees.

Kirsty twisted round to look at her back. She had wings – shiny and delicate as a butterfly's!

Ruby beamed at them. "Now you can fly," she said. "Let's go."

Rachel twitched her shoulders. Her wings fluttered, and she felt herself rise up into the air. She felt quite wobbly at first. It was very odd!

"Help!" Kirsty yelled, as she shot up into the air. "I'm not very good at this!"

"Come on," said Ruby, taking their hands. "I'll help you." She led them up, out of the glade.

Rachel looked down on Rainspell Island. She could see the cottages next to the beach, and the harbour.

"Where *is* Fairyland, Ruby?" Kirsty asked. They were flying higher and higher, up into the clouds.

"It's so far away that no mortal could ever find it," Ruby said.

They flew on through the clouds for a long, long time. But at last Ruby turned to them and smiled. "We're here," she said.

As they flew down from the clouds, Kirsty and Rachel saw places they recognised from the pond picture: the palace, the hillsides with their toadstool houses, the river and flowers. But there were no bright colours now. Because of Jack Frost's spell, everything was a drab shade of grey. Even the air felt cold and damp.

A few fairies walked miserably across the hillsides. Their wings hung limply down their backs. No one could be bothered to fly.

Suddenly, one of the fairies looked up into the sky. "Look!" she shouted. "It's Ruby. She's come back!"

At once, the fairies flew up towards Ruby, Kirsty and Rachel. They circled around them, looking much happier, and asking lots of questions.

"Have you come from Rainspell, Ruby?"

"Where are the other Rainbow Fairies?"

"Who are your friends?"

"First, we must see the King and Queen. Then I will tell you everything!" Ruby promised.

King Oberon and Queen Titania were seated on their thrones. Their palace was as grey and gloomy as everywhere else in Fairyland. But they smiled warmly when Ruby arrived with Rachel and Kirsty.

"Welcome back, Ruby," the Queen said. "We have missed you."

"Your Majesties, I have found two mortals who believe in magic!" Ruby announced. "These are my friends, Kirsty and Rachel."

Quickly Ruby explained what had happened to the other Rainbow Fairies. She told everyone how Rachel and Kirsty had rescued her.

"You have our thanks," the King told them. "Our Rainbow Fairies are very special to us."

"And will you help us to find Ruby's Rainbow sisters?" the Queen asked.

"Yes, we will," Kirsty said.

"But how will we know where to look?" Rachel wanted to know.

"The trick is not to look too hard," said Queen Titania. "Don't worry. As you enjoy the rest of your holiday, the magic you need to find each Rainbow Fairy will find *you*. Just wait and see."

King Oberon rubbed his beard thoughtfully.

"You have six days of your holiday left, and six fairies to find," he said. "A fairy each day. That's a lot of fairy-finding. You will need some special help." He nodded at one of his footmen, a plump frog in a buttoned-up jacket.

The frog hopped over to Rachel and Kirsty and handed them each a tiny, silver bag.

"The bags contain magic tools," the Queen told them. "Don't look inside them yet. Open them only when you really need to, and you will find something to help you." She smiled at Kirsty and Rachel.

"Look!" shouted another frog footman suddenly. "Ruby is beginning to fade!"

Rachel and Kirsty looked at Ruby in horror. The fairy was growing paler before their eyes. Her lovely dress was no longer red but pink, and her golden hair was turning white.

"Jack Frost's magic is still at work," said the King, looking worried. "We cannot undo his spell until the Rainbow Fairies are all together again."

"Quickly, Ruby!" urged the Queen. "You must return to Rainspell at once."

Ruby, Kirsty and Rachel rose into the air, their wings fluttering.

"Don't worry!" Kirsty called, as they flew higher. "We'll be back with all the Rainbow Fairies very soon!"

"Good luck!" called the King and Queen.

Rachel and Kirsty watched Ruby worriedly as they flew off. But as they got further away from Fairyland, Ruby's colour began to return. Soon she was bright and sparkling again.

They reached Rainspell at last. Ruby led Rachel and Kirsty to the clearing in the wood, and they landed next to the old black pot. Then Ruby scattered fairy dust over Rachel and Kirsty.

There was a puff of glittering red smoke, and the two girls shot up to their normal size again.

Rachel wriggled her shoulders. Yes, her wings had gone.

"Oh, I really *loved* being a fairy," Kirsty said.

They watched as Ruby sprinkled her magic dust over the old black pot.

"What are you doing?" Rachel asked.

"Jack Frost's magic means that I can't help you look for my sisters," Ruby replied sadly. "So I will wait for you here, in the pot at the end of the rainbow."

Suddenly the pot began to move. It rolled across the grass, and stopped under the weeping willow tree. The tree's branches hung right down to the ground.

"The pot will be hidden under the tree," Ruby explained. "I'll be safe there."

"We'd better start looking for the other Rainbow Fairies," Rachel said to Kirsty. "Where shall we start?"

Ruby shook her head. "Remember what the Queen said," she told them. "The magic will come to you." She flew over and sat on the edge of the pot. Then she pushed aside one of the willow branches and waved at Rachel and Kirsty. "Goodbye, and good luck!"

"We'll be back soon, Ruby," Kirsty promised.

"We're going to find all your Rainbow sisters," Rachel said firmly. "Just you wait and see!"

Meet Ruby the Red Fairy

Ruby the Red Fairy is extra-special as she's the first fairy that Kirsty and Rachel ever met on Rainspell Island!

Happiest hobby

Flying as fast as she can over Fairyland, performing tricks and tumbles.

Personality

Feisty, high-spirited and full of fun.

Fairy playmates

The Dance Fairies and the Sporty Fairies.

Although she is lighter than a butterfly, Ruby will do anything and go anywhere to help a friend in trouble!

Favourite colour

Bright red, the colour of courage and energy.

Yummiest food

Raspberry jelly and strawberry milkshake.

Fairy outfit

Ruby's beautiful dress is the colour of fresh strawberries. She plaits her golden hair with tiny red rose buds and pops crimson slippers on her feet. Her little earrings and locket were a present from Queen Titania.

Show What You Know!

Friendship is the most important thing in Fairyland, and the Rainbow Magic fairies have devised this quiz to work out how well you know your best friend! Sit on your own and try to answer as many questions as you can. When you've finished, ask your best friend to mark your answers and total up your scores.

What does she like for breakfast?

Which clubs does she belong to?

What colour are your friend's eyes?

What outfit is she most likely to wear?

What's her favourite pop group?

Where did she last go on holiday?

What's her best subject at school?

What is her favourite colour?

What colour is her bedroom?

What's the name of her oldest cuddly toy?

What's her scrummiest food?

What's on her pencil case?

Scores 0-6

It's a promising start, but there's so much more to discover about your best friend! It's time to do lots more listening to find out all the things that make her tick.

Scores 7-13

Your friend still holds a few secrets, but maybe you're still getting to know each other? Keep chatting and sharing and you'll have full points in no time!

Scores 14-20

Well done, you really do know your friend inside out! You take the fairy friendship promise very seriously, and clearly share everything together.

Kylie the Carnival Fairy

Fairy magic means carnival fun
While the magic hats are where they belong.
But my icy spells will cause a stir
When those hats are no longer where they were!

Band Leader's hat and Carnival Crown
Both will go missing when I come to town.
But I'll start with the Carnival Master's hat
And send my goblin servants to capture that!

Kylie the Carnival Fairy helps make carnivals fun for everyone! But when Jack Frost and his goblins pay a visit to the Sunnydays Carnival, they look sure to spoil the fun...

Carnival Hat Hijinks

Contents

The Carnival Begins

"This is exciting!" Rachel Walker exclaimed to her best friend, Kirsty Tate. "I've never been to a carnival before."

"Sunnydays is the best carnival of them all," Kirsty replied. "It visits Wetherbury every year at the end of the summer holidays. I'm so glad you're staying with us, so that you can come too."

The girls were standing with Kirsty's parents and a large crowd of people outside the gates of the carnival showground. There was a buzz of excited chatter as everyone waited for the Grand Opening.

"Which ride will you go on first, girls?" asked Mr Tate.

"I don't know," Kirsty said, peering through the gates. "There are so many!" She could see a Ferris wheel, dodgems, spinning teacups and many more. There were also stalls offering sweets and games like hoopla and hook-a-duck.

"Look, Kirsty!" Rachel nudged her friend as a man in a red coat and a black top hat appeared behind the gates.

"He must be the Carnival Master," Kirsty explained. "It's time for the Grand Opening!"

The crowd cheered loudly.

"Ladies and gentlemen," boomed the Carnival Master. "Welcome to Sunnydays, the most magical carnival in the world!" And he threw open the gates with a flourish.

"Follow me!"

Rachel and Kirsty hurried inside the showground eagerly, along with the rest of the crowd.

"Let the carnival magic begin!" announced the Carnival Master, sweeping off his top hat and pointing it at the Ferris wheel. Immediately the great wheel began to turn. The crowd gasped.

Then the Carnival Master waved his hat at the teacups, which began to spin in a blur of bright colours.

"It *is* magic!" gasped a little girl near Kirsty, as the rides sprang to life. Rachel and Kirsty smiled. They knew all about magic. The two girls had become friends with the fairies, and helped their tiny friends whenever cold, spiteful Jack Frost and his goblin servants were causing trouble.

A loud drumbeat echoed through the air.

"It's the parade!" Kirsty cried.

There was a clash of cymbals and a band, led by a man in a smart uniform, marched towards the crowd. The Band Leader wore a green peaked cap, trimmed with gold braid, and carried a red and white baton. As the spectators cheered, he tipped his hat to them and twirled his baton. Immediately, the band struck up a merry tune.

"This is great," Rachel said as the band marched past. "Look, there are dancers and acrobats."

Behind the band came dancers in blue and pink dresses, with long satin ribbons in their hands that they twirled and twisted as they danced. Acrobats jumped and tumbled, handing out party poppers in between cartwheels. Kirsty and Rachel were delighted to get one each.

"There are jugglers too!" Kirsty pointed out.

The jugglers wore jester's hats with bells on, and carried colourful juggling balls.

"Oh, dear!" Rachel sighed, as one of the jugglers dropped all his balls at once. "I think they need a bit more practice."

Kirsty frowned as another of the jugglers stumbled into one of the acrobats. "They're not very tall, are they?" she said. "Perhaps they're children. That would explain why they're not very good at juggling yet." But then Kirsty glanced down at the jugglers' feet. Their shoes were huge – much too big for children's shoes!

Kirsty peered closely at the jugglers as they paraded past. Although their hats hid most of their faces, she could just make out that they had long, green noses.

"Rachel!" Kirsty whispered, her heart pounding. "Those jugglers aren't children. They're goblins!"

Goblins Make Mischief

"Oh, no!" Rachel gasped, realising Kirsty was right.

"Why are Jack Frost's goblins here?" Kirsty wondered, counting them quickly. "Rachel, there are eight of them!"

"And Jack Frost has made them bigger too," Rachel added. "They're almost as tall as us. That must be so that they don't stand out in the crowd."

"I bet they're up to no good!" Kirsty said, frowning.

"Now, let me present our most magical ride," the Carnival Master was saying.

"Look at the goblins," Kirsty whispered.

All eight goblins were dashing straight towards the Carnival Master. As they got close to him, the biggest goblin suddenly jumped up and knocked the top hat off his head!

The Carnival Master cried out in surprise, but everyone else laughed, thinking it was part of the show. One of the other goblins caught the hat as it fell, and then they all disappeared into the crowd.

"Why do the goblins want the Carnival Master's hat?" Kirsty asked, as the shocked Carnival Master struggled to continue with his announcement.

"Er, as I was saying," he stammered. "This is the most important ride of the carnival!" He pointed at a huge green sheet, which was clearly screening something very large.

Two clowns on stilts stood either side of the sheet, each holding a corner. There was a drum roll from the band, and then the clowns pulled the sheet away to reveal a brightly-painted carousel of elegant, high-stepping horses – but unlike the other rides, this one didn't start turning.

"The carousel will be working soon," the Carnival Master said hastily. "Meanwhile, please enjoy our other wonderful rides!"

But as Kirsty and Rachel looked around the showground, they saw that the Ferris wheel seemed to be stopping, and the teacups were slowing to a halt too.

Suddenly, out of the corner of her eye, Kirsty caught a flash of purple. It was the goblins again. And this time they were rushing towards the Band Leader.

"Look out!" Kirsty cried, trying to warn him.

But the band was playing too loudly for him to hear her.

Once again the tallest goblin jumped up and knocked the hat off the Band Leader's head. Another goblin swept it up off the ground, and all the goblins raced away.

The instant the Band Leader lost his hat, he also lost control of the band. The tubas and flutes sounded out of time, the trumpeters started marching in the wrong direction and the drummers dropped their drumsticks. The tuneful music became a deafening din.

"Why are the goblins trying to spoil the carnival?" Rachel wondered.

"I don't know," Kirsty sighed.

The band had stopped playing now, and the Band Leader was looking dazed. The Carnival Master rushed forwards. "Don't forget," he announced, "for the Closing Day Parade, we want you all to come in fancy dress. The boy

or girl with the best costume will be crowned Carnival King or Queen with our splendid Carnival Crown!"

Just then Rachel and Kirsty heard the clip-clop of hooves behind them. Everyone turned to see two women in sparkly costumes riding ponies. The women carried a blue velvet cushion between them, and on top of the cushion sat the Carnival Crown, studded with gems and feathers.

"And now I declare Sunnydays Carnival officially open!" the Carnival Master cried proudly.

The crowd cheered and scattered to explore the carnival.

"We must find out what the goblins are up to," Rachel said anxiously.

Kirsty nodded, beginning to shiver. "It's suddenly got cold, hasn't it?" she said, her teeth chattering.

Rachel nodded and rubbed her arms. "It's been warm all day until now," she said, frowning.

At that moment Kirsty noticed a clown in a baggy costume and curly purple wig standing nearby. He was staring intently at the Carnival Crown.

Kirsty nudged Rachel. "Look," she whispered. "There's something familiar about that clown."

Rachel stared at the clown. Then, with a start, she noticed frosty icicles hanging from his chin. "Kirsty," Rachel gasped. "That's Jack Frost!"

Kylie Pops In

Kirsty stared at Jack Frost in horror. "He's used his magic to make himself as big as the goblins," she whispered to Rachel. At that moment, the goblins suddenly reappeared. Trying to juggle, they quickly surrounded the Carnival Crown.

Meanwhile Jack Frost had conjured up an icy wind that swept him up and carried him through the air. Only Kirsty and Rachel noticed as he zoomed towards the crown; everybody else was too busy watching the goblin jugglers.

The girls stared in dismay as Jack Frost snatched the crown from its cushion and zoomed away out of sight. Immediately, the goblins gathered up their juggling balls and hurried after him. Rachel and Kirsty tried to follow, but the goblins disappeared too quickly.

"The crown!" gasped one of the women on the ponies. "Where did it go?"

"Maybe it fell off the cushion," the other suggested, and they began looking around for it.

"Now Jack Frost has the Carnival Master's hat, the Band Leader's hat and the Carnival Crown!" Kirsty said anxiously.

"What's he going to do with them?"

"Let's go and see," Rachel suggested.

Kirsty turned to her parents, who were chatting to some friends. "Mum, can Rachel and I go on the rides?"

Mrs Tate nodded. "We'll meet you at the gates in half an hour," she replied. The girls hurried after the goblins.

Suddenly, Rachel felt a tingling in her fingers. She glanced down to see that she was still holding her party popper. And now it seemed to be shaking all by itself!

Suddenly the party popper exploded in a shower of glitter. Rachel jumped as streamers shot into the air. "Oh!" she said in surprise.

A fairy was hovering amid the streamers, beaming at the girls. As the streamers floated to the ground, the fairy flew to Kirsty's shoulder. Her skirt, striped in all the colours of the rainbow, billowed around her as she landed.

"Hello, girls!" the fairy called, pushing a few strands of her dark brown hair out of her eyes. "I'm Kylie the Carnival Fairy!"

"Hello," Rachel gasped.

"It's my job to make sure the Sunnydays Carnival is a huge success," Kylie explained. "But Jack Frost is trying to ruin everything!"

"Why?" asked Kirsty.

"Because he got bored in his ice castle," Kylie sighed. "And so he's decided to spoil everybody's fun."

"What about the hats?" Rachel wanted to know.

Kylie winked at the girls.

"The hats are magical!" she said with a grin. "The Carnival Master's hat makes sure all the rides run smoothly."

"No wonder the carousel wasn't working," Kirsty said.

Kylie nodded. "The magic of the Band Leader's hat makes the carnival music perfect," she went on. "That's why the band can't play in tune anymore.

And the Carnival Crown makes sure that Sunnydays Carnival ends happily and can move on to the next town."

"So if we can't get the hats back, the carnival will be ruined for everyone!" Rachel cried.

"We can't let that happen," Kirsty added.

"I knew you'd help me, girls," Kylie declared happily. "Now, where are Jack Frost and his goblins?"

"They went that way," Rachel said.

As the girls looked in that direction, Kirsty spotted a flash of purple.

"There's a goblin," she said excitedly, pointing him out to Rachel and Kylie. "And he's got the Carnival Master's hat!"

"After him!" Kylie cried, sliding into Rachel's pocket, out of sight.

The girls hurried towards the goblin, but before they could reach him, he spotted them.

"It's those pesky girls!" he shouted to his two companions. "Quick, hide!"

The three goblins immediately dashed off, closely followed by the girls.

As the goblins passed the ghost train, one of them skidded to a halt. "In here!" he shouted. Ignoring the "Broken – Please Come Back Later" sign, the three goblins rushed inside.

Kirsty and Rachel blinked as they saw a shimmer of magic, and suddenly all the lights outside the ghost train came on.

"The magic of the Carnival Master's hat is making the ride work," Kylie explained.

The giggling goblins climbed into the front carriage of the train, and Rachel and Kirsty just managed to jump into the carriage behind as the train pulled away.

As the train turned the corner, the girls saw spiders' webs and bats hanging from dark trees. A cold wind howled around them. Rachel and Kirsty knew it was only a sound effect, but the goblins had stopped giggling and

were muttering to each other in scared voices.

"*Whoooooooo!*" A ghost jumped out from behind a tree, moaning loudly.

The goblins shrieked with fright.

"I don't think the goblins are enjoying the ride!" Kirsty laughed.

As the train rattled round another corner, a loud creaking sound filled the air.

"What's that?" the goblins wailed. Then they screamed in terror as a coffin swung open, and a vampire with long sharp fangs leant out to grab them.

Eventually, the train shot through the doors and came to a stop. Still moaning with fright, the goblins leapt out of the train and ran away.

"They're heading for the Log Falls ride," Kylie said. "Quick!"

The Log Falls ride wasn't working. It had a "No Entry" sign outside. But, once again, the goblins ignored the sign and jumped into one of the floating, log-shaped boats. Immediately, there was a dazzling flash of magic.

"The Carnival Master's hat's at work again," Rachel said.

Sure enough, water was beginning to tumble and splash along the waterways, and the goblins' little boat floated away.

Kirsty turned to Rachel and Kylie. "What are we going to do?" she asked.

Rachel was staring at the waterways. "I've got an idea!" she announced.

Goblins Outwitted!

"What is it?" Kylie asked eagerly.

"Look!" Rachel pointed at the ride. At the bottom of one of the waterways was a long slide.

"The goblins will be coming down that slide soon," Rachel explained. "If we stand at the bottom, we can try to grab the hat as they go past."

"Perfect!" Kylie exclaimed.

The goblins were out of sight on one of the other waterways, but the girls and Kylie could hear them squealing with delight. Quickly they hurried over to the bottom of the slide and waited.

"They're at the top of the slide," Rachel whispered, as the goblins' boat floated into sight. "Get ready!"

At that moment, the log boat tipped over the edge and shot down the slide towards the girls.

"Yee-hah!" the goblins yelled, waving their arms in the air. They were sitting one behind the other in the little boat. Rachel, Kirsty and Kylie could see that the goblin with the Carnival Master's hat was right at the back.

The boat zoomed down to the bottom of the slide. Kirsty was closest to the waterway,

and as the boat splashed past, she reached out and snatched the hat right out of the astonished goblin's grasp!

"Give that back!" the goblin yelled furiously as he was carried past. "Stop the boat!" But there was nothing the goblins could do. The boat swept on along the waterways, taking the angry goblins with it.

"Well done!" laughed Kylie, as Kirsty shook drops of water off the hat. "Now, let's take it back to where it belongs."

Kylie slipped into Rachel's pocket again, and they all hurried off to the main tent, a huge white marquee in the middle of the showground. The Carnival Master was standing in the entrance with the Band Leader, looking very unhappy.

"I think we might have to close the carnival," the Carnival Master was saying. "Too many rides aren't working!"

"We're just in time," Kirsty whispered.

"But how are we going to give the hat back?" Rachel asked. "They'll want to know where we found it!"

"Kylie, could you make us fairy-sized?" Kirsty asked quietly.

"And the hat too?" added Rachel. "Then we'll be able to return it without being seen."

Kylie nodded. Quickly the girls slipped behind the tent, where Kylie waved her wand over them. Rachel, Kirsty and the hat immediately

shrank to fairy-size. Then, carrying the tiny hat, the girls and Kylie flew back to the tent entrance.

They waited until the Carnival Master went to check on the rides, then they flew inside and put the hat on his desk. Immediately, Kylie waved her wand again and the hat shot back to its usual size. Then they fluttered back outside, and Kylie's magic soon turned Rachel and Kirsty into normal girls again.

A moment later, they heard the Carnival Master returning to the tent.

"We'll have to close down," he said to the Band Leader. "I'll make an announcement."

Kirsty, Rachel and Kylie peeped round the side of the tent as the Carnival Master went inside.

"My hat!" he exclaimed in surprise. "How did that get there?" And he picked it up and put it on.

Rachel and Kirsty beamed at each other as suddenly, all around them, they heard the whirr and purr of rides starting up again. The Ferris wheel was moving, the teacups started spinning and the dodgems were soon bumping into each other.

"Look, even the carousel's turning!" Rachel pointed out.

"Everything's working again!" the Band Leader exclaimed in amazement.

"That's wonderful!" the Carnival Master gasped, rushing out of the tent to see. "It's almost like magic!"

Kylie laughed as she turned to Rachel and Kirsty. "It *is* magic, girls!" she said. "And I couldn't have got the magic hat back without

you." She smiled at them. "Now I must be off to Fairyland to tell everyone the good news."

"We'd better go and find my mum and dad," Kirsty said.

Rachel nodded. "But we'll be back tomorrow to help you find the other hats," she promised Kylie.

"Thank you, girls," Kylie called, waving as she disappeared in a dazzling shower of sparkles.

"What a meanie Jack Frost is," said Kirsty, as she and Rachel headed for the gates. "He hates to see people having fun."

"Well, we won't let him spoil the carnival!" Rachel said in a determined voice. "I wonder if we'll find another hat tomorrow?"

Musical Muddle

Contents

Mirror Magic

"I'm glad Mum and Dad let us come to Sunnydays Carnival early today," Kirsty remarked, as she and Rachel walked round the carnival ground. It was the second day of the carnival and it was sunny again with clear blue skies. "It gives us more time to look for the magic hats."

"Well, you did tell them we wanted to go on all the rides!" Rachel said with a grin.

"Yes, but Dad says we must meet up later so that we can all go on the roller coaster together," laughed Kirsty. "That's his favourite."

Suddenly, a terrible din made Rachel clap her hands over her ears. "What's that noise?" she cried. "It's horrible!"

"It's the band," Kirsty said sadly. "No wonder it sounds awful – they don't have the magic of the Band Leader's hat to make sure all the music goes smoothly!"

"Look!" Rachel pointed at the stage. "The dancers are putting on a show. That's why the band's playing."

The girls walked towards the stage, but as they got closer, they saw that nothing was going right. Not only was the band playing out of tune, but it was out of time too. The dancers couldn't keep in step, so they kept bumping into each other.

"The Band Leader looks very upset," whispered Kirsty.

Rachel saw that the Band Leader was conducting the music, and wincing at every wrong note. Only a few people were watching the show, and some of them had their fingers in their ears.

Just then, the Carnival Master hurried onto the stage, looking flustered. "Thank you, dancers," he said loudly, "The show's over, ladies and gentlemen!" And he began to clap. A few members of the audience clapped too, but rather half-heartedly, as they began to move away. The Carnival Master shook his head in despair. "I don't know what's going on," he said, staring at the dancers.

"You're usually so good!" He sighed. "Come along, you need a break. I'll take you to the refreshments tent for tea and biscuits."

Looking glum, the dancers trailed off the stage.

"I think you'd better go too," the Band Leader said, looking sadly at his musicians. "We'll try again later."

"The music won't sound right till we get the Band Leader's hat back," Kirsty said as she and Rachel watched the gloomy musicians put down their instruments and leave.

"Maybe we should start looking for it right away," Rachel suggested. "I bet the goblins are still around here somewhere, enjoying the carnival."

"Oh, but remember what the fairies always say," Kirsty grinned at her. "We must let the magic come to us!"

Rachel laughed. "In that case, why don't we have some carnival fun ourselves?" she said.

"Good idea," Kirsty agreed.

The girls wandered round the showground, enjoying the sunshine. They passed a fancy dress and face-painting tent, and a man selling candyfloss. Next door was the Hall of Mirrors.

"Oh, I love this!" Rachel said eagerly. "Let's go in."

Kirsty swung the door open, and the girls stepped inside.

For a split second it was dark, but as the door closed, the lights came on. Immediately the girls were surrounded by hundreds of Kirstys and Rachels, reflected in the tall mirrors all around them!

"This is weird," Rachel laughed, turning this way and that. Her reflections turned this way and that too. "Look, Kirsty." She raised her arms, and hundreds of Rachels raised their arms too.

Before Kirsty could speak, there was a sudden pop, and a burst of multicoloured glitter appeared in midair and surrounded the girls as it floated to the ground.

"Where did that come from?" Kirsty gasped in surprise and delight. The glitter reflected in all the mirrors, making the girls feel as if they were surrounded by dazzling fireworks.

"Look," Rachel cried. "Fairies!"

There, dancing in the mirrors, the girls could see hundreds of tiny fairies, their wings fluttering and shimmering with light. It was such a magical sight that Kirsty and Rachel could hardly believe their eyes!

Then Rachel laughed. "Oh, look, it's not hundreds of fairies," she told Kirsty. "It's Kylie!"

Suspicious Scouts

"Hello, girls!" called a silvery voice behind them, and the girls turned to see Kylie smiling happily. "I'm so glad to see you," she went on. "I can sense that the Band Leader's hat isn't far away!"

"Great!" Kirsty said eagerly. "Let's keep our eyes open."

"First we have to find the way out of here," said Rachel, looking around in confusion at all the mirrors.

"The exit door must have a mirror on the back to hide it," Kirsty said with a frown.

"I'll help," Kylie said, smiling and waving her wand. A shower of magic pink sparkles flew from the wand and surrounded one of the mirrors in a glittering frame of fairy dust.

Rachel hurried over and pushed the mirror. It swung open, and as the girls made their way outside, Kylie flew down to Kirsty's shoulder and hid behind her hair.

Kirsty and Rachel stood outside the Hall of Mirrors looking around. Rachel turned and saw the fancy-dress tent. A group of Cub Scouts in their dark green uniforms were gathered just inside, squealing with delight as they tried on different outfits and had their faces painted.

Rachel was about to turn away, when she suddenly realised that something wasn't quite right. For one thing, there were no carnival people at the tent – the Boy Scouts were painting each other's faces! Rachel stared a little harder.

"Look at those Scouts," she said to Kirsty and Kylie.

Kirsty and the little fairy turned to look. At that moment, one of the Scouts, who was dressed as a witch, rushed forwards and pushed another, who was still in his Scout uniform but had an orange and black stripy tiger's face, out of the face-painting chair.

"It's my turn now!" yelled the first Scout, sitting down and whipping off his witch's hat. Now Kylie, Rachel and Kirsty could all see that his face was green!

"He's a goblin!" Rachel breathed.

"They're all goblins!" Kirsty added.

The girls edged closer to the tent. They could see that the goblins had been very busy. One was dressed in a monkey suit, with a monkey mask. And another was wearing a black suit with bones on it so that he looked like a skeleton! Rachel noticed that his face had been scarily painted to look like a skull.

"Look at the one doing the painting!" Kirsty whispered to Rachel and Kylie. They couldn't help laughing when they saw that the goblin looked exactly like Jack Frost! He wore a cloak round his shoulders and had a spiky wig and beard, which he had clearly painted white to look like Jack Frost's icy hair.

He was glaring at the witch goblin who had sat down to have his face painted. "You don't need painting!" he snapped. "Everybody knows witches are supposed to be green."

Suddenly, through the open doorway of the tent, Rachel spotted the Band Leader's green and gold hat on the table. "There's the hat!" she whispered excitedly, pointing it out.

"Girls, if I make you fairy-sized, perhaps we can slip in and get the hat back without being spotted," Kylie whispered.

Rachel and Kirsty nodded, Kylie waved her wand, and soon the girls were tiny fairies with glittering wings on their backs. Then all three friends flew cautiously towards the fancy-dress tent.

Frightening Faces

Just before the friends reached the entrance, the tiger-faced goblin hurried over to the table. To the girls' dismay, he grabbed the Band Leader's hat and jammed it firmly on his head. Then he marched out of the tent.

"After him!" whispered Kirsty.

The tiger-faced goblin started to hurry off across the showground.

"Where are you going?" the skeleton goblin shouted after him.

The goblin stuck his tongue out. "I'm going to have some fun on the rides!" he yelled. He looked very silly in his Scout uniform, with his tiger's face, the Band Leader's hat perched on his head, and his tongue sticking out! Rachel, Kylie and Kirsty couldn't help laughing.

"I want to have fun too!" roared the skeleton goblin, dropping the pirate costume he'd been about to try on.

"So do we!" shouted the other goblins, throwing down the paint tubes and bits of costumes they were holding.

"Let's go!" Rachel whispered. And the three friends flew after the goblins, wondering which ride they would head for.

But the tiger-faced goblin stopped when he saw the "Hall of Mirrors" sign. "What's a hall of mirrors?" he asked.

"Oh, you are silly!" scoffed the goblin in the monkey suit. "Everyone knows what a hall of mirrors is!"

"Well, what is it?" asked the first goblin.

"It's…er…" The monkey-faced goblin's voice trailed away and he looked very uncomfortable.

"He doesn't know!" scoffed the wicked witch goblin. "Let's go inside and find out!" He pulled open the door and the goblins began fighting to get in first.

"We'll slip inside before they close the door," Kylie whispered to the girls. "One, two, three, go!"

As the door swung shut, Kylie, Rachel and Kirsty swooped forwards and managed to dart inside.

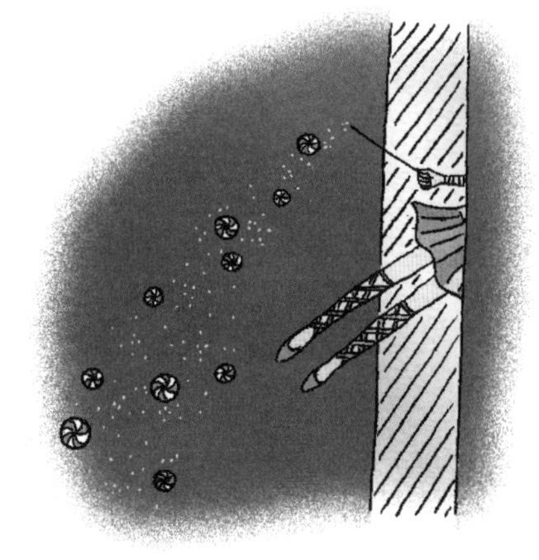

Just as before, the lights came on as soon as the door closed. Hovering high overhead, Rachel, Kirsty and Kylie could see the goblins' painted faces reflected hundreds of times in the mirrors. The goblins could see them too, and they stared at the mirrors in alarm.

"Help!" shrieked the tiger-faced goblin. "Where have all these scary monsters come from?"

"Get me out of here!" roared the Jack Frost goblin. "I can see hundreds of tigers!"

"Uh-oh, Jack Frost's here – dozens of him!" the monkey-faced goblin yelled in terror. "And he looks really angry!"

Kirsty turned to Kylie and Rachel. "The goblins don't realise they're looking at their own reflections," she laughed. "They're scaring themselves silly!"

"I can see skeletons!" moaned the wicked witch goblin. "Hundreds of horrible skeletons come to life!"

He backed away from the mirrors and cannoned straight into the tiger-faced goblin.

They bumped into each other so hard that the Band Leader's hat fell off. Suddenly the tiger-faced goblin gave a shout. "Hey! Those monsters aren't monsters!" he gasped. "They're us!" And he pointed at the mirror nearest him.

"The tiger's pointing at us!" gasped the monkey-suited goblin in terror.

"That's because it's ME!" the tiger-faced goblin shouted impatiently. "It's my reflection!"

Kirsty was laughing so hard she thought she would burst, and Kylie was giggling too. But

Rachel was staring at the hat lying on the floor. "Now's our chance," she whispered. "Together we can lift it!"

Kylie and Kirsty stopped laughing and nodded as the goblins stared more closely at the mirrors and finally realised what the tiger-faced goblin had been telling them.

"I knew it all along!" said the Jack Frost goblin. "What a lot of silly fools you are!"

"Who are you calling a fool?" snapped the tiger-faced goblin.

Rachel, Kirsty and Kylie fluttered down over the goblins' heads towards the hat, but just as they were almost within reach, the tiger-faced goblin snatched it up! Kylie and the girls had to zoom behind a mirror to hide.

"I've found the door!" yelled the wicked witch goblin, suddenly, pushing it open. The goblins tumbled out into the sunshine, still arguing loudly, and the door slammed shut behind them.

This time Kylie and the girls weren't quick enough to fly out.

"We nearly had the hat that time!" Rachel sighed.

"We mustn't give up," Kirsty said firmly. "Kylie, can you make us human-sized again so we can open the door?"

Kylie nodded, and in a shower of magic sparkles from her wand, the girls shot up to their normal size. Then they raced out of the Hall of Mirrors with Kylie perched on Rachel's shoulder.

"There go the goblins!" Rachel said, pointing ahead.

"It looks like they're heading for the teacups," added Kirsty.

The girls hurried after them. The carnival was even busier now than it had been earlier, and all the rides the girls passed were full, including the carousel. Rachel smiled to see children sitting on the pretty wooden horses, beaming happily as they whizzed round and round. But then she frowned. "The carousel music sounds awfully tinny and out of tune!" she remarked.

"So does the music on the dodgems," Kirsty agreed, as they hurried on past the bumper cars.

"Music is very important in making sure everyone enjoys the carnival," Kylie sighed. "That's why we must get the Band Leader's hat back soon!"

Giddy Goblins!

The goblins were looking excited as they headed for a large pink teacup. They all climbed in and waited for the ride to start.

"What now?" asked Rachel, staring at the tiger-faced goblin, who was still wearing the magic hat.

Kirsty had been thinking hard. "I've got an idea," she said slowly, as the ride started up. "Kylie, could you make the teacup spin even faster than usual?"

Kylie's eyes twinkled. "Oh, yes," she replied.

The goblins were enjoying themselves as the ride turned and their teacup began to spin. Smiling, Kylie pointed her wand at the goblins' cup and sent sparkling fairy dust rushing towards it. The teacup began to spin faster.

"Hurrah!" shouted the goblins. "This is fun!"

"That's not fast enough!" Kylie laughed, and she waved her wand again. Now the teacup began to whizz round even more quickly. Rachel and Kirsty could see that the goblins were starting to look woozy and even greener than usual!

The teacup was now moving so fast that the tiger-faced goblin was forced to hang on to the side. Kylie raised her wand one last time, and a shower of sparkles made the teacup spin super-fast, so that the goblins were almost a blur.

The witch's hat was on tightly, but the Band Leader's hat wasn't. The tiger-faced goblin put up a hand to hold the Band Leader's hat on, but he was too late. It flew off his head and went spinning through the air.

"My hat!" the tiger-faced goblin shrieked.

"Stop the teacup!" moaned the wicked witch goblin. "I want to get off!"

Rachel hurried over and picked up the hat, as Kylie lifted her wand to slow the teacup down again. Then the girls watched as the ride stopped and the goblins climbed off. They were so dizzy that they couldn't walk straight. Rachel giggled as they bumped into each other.

"Thank goodness we've got the hat back," said Kylie. "But now we must take it to the Band Leader. It's almost time for the afternoon show."

They hurried off to the tent next to the stage. The Band Leader was standing outside with the Carnival Master, and as the girls and Kylie approached, they could hear them talking.

"It's time for the show," the Carnival Master was saying. "Look, there are lots of people in the audience and the dancers and the band have had a break now. I'm sure they'll be much better."

The Band Leader nodded, but he looked rather doubtful as he went into the tent where his musicians were tuning their instruments.

Rachel, Kirsty and Kylie followed. They peeped through the tent flap and saw the band lining up with the dancers behind them.

"How are we going to give the hat back?" Rachel whispered.

"The Band Leader hasn't picked up his baton yet," Kirsty said, noticing it on the table. "Kylie, maybe you could make the hat appear right next to it?"

Kylie winked. With a flick of her wand she made the hat shrink. Then she sent the tiny hat whizzing through the tent flap and over the table. It landed neatly next to the baton. With a final wave of her wand, Kylie made it grow back to its normal size.

"Perfect!" Kirsty beamed.

The band leader hurried over to the table to pick up his baton, but he stopped in surprise as he saw his hat lying next to it. "My hat!" he gasped. "How did that get there?" Smiling from ear to ear, the Band Leader put his hat on, picked his baton up and cleared his throat.

"Now, let's try to play a bit better than earlier, shall we?" he said to the band.

Looking rather nervous, the Band Leader took his place at the head of the parade and raised his baton. The trumpeters played a fanfare as they all marched towards the tent opening. Rachel, Kirsty and Kylie drew back to watch the parade.

The band broke into a lively tune, played in perfect time, and the girls grinned at each other. On stage, the dancers twirled their batons and

performed their steps expertly, never missing a beat. The audience began to applaud loudly.

"Everything is back to normal!" Rachel said with a sigh of relief, turning to glance at the carousel. The horses were still spinning, and the music sounded sweet and tuneful now.

"Not quite everything!" Kylie replied. "The goblins still have the Carnival Crown. And without that, the carnival won't be able to move on to the next town, which means lots of other boys and girls will miss out!"

"Don't worry, Kylie," Kirsty said. "We'll do our best to find the crown."

Kylie smiled gratefully. "Thank you," she said. "But it's your carnival too! So go and enjoy yourselves now, while I return to Fairyland and tell the King and Queen the latest news. They'll be so pleased to hear we've only one magical hat left to find!" She waved her wand in farewell. "See you tomorrow!"

Rachel and Kirsty waved as Kylie disappeared in a shower of sparkles.

"It's time to meet Mum and Dad at the roller coaster," said Kirsty.

"Well, Kylie did tell us to go and enjoy ourselves," Rachel replied with a grin. "And tomorrow, we'll be on the lookout for the Carnival Crown!"

Carnival Crown

Contents

Cats and Clowns

"I can't believe it's the last day of the carnival!" Kirsty said, slipping on her eye mask. "How do I look, Rachel?"

"Brilliant!" Rachel laughed.

Both girls were wearing their fancy-dress costumes, ready for the Closing Day Parade.

The parade and a fireworks display were taking place that evening, but the girls had visited the carnival earlier in the day, hoping to find the missing Carnival Crown.

Unfortunately, they hadn't seen a single goblin or any sign of the stolen crown.

Rachel and Kirsty were dressed as black cats in black trousers, black jumpers and black velvet eye masks. Mrs Tate had made them a fluffy tail each, and the girls had drawn whiskers on their faces with black eyeliner.

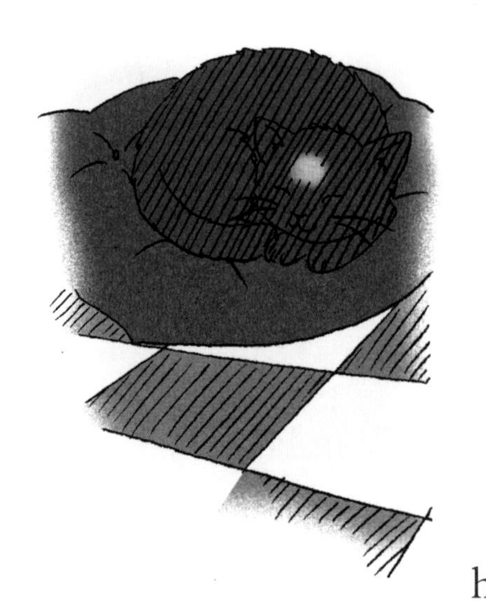

"Pearl doesn't look impressed!" Kirsty laughed, glancing at her cat, who was snoozing on her bed.

Rachel smiled, then frowned nervously. "I'm looking forward to the parade, but I'm worried," he said. "If we don't find the crown, Sunnydays Carnival won't be able to finish properly and move on to the next town."

Kirsty nodded. "Let's hope we have some luck tonight," she said.

"Are you ready, girls?" Mr Tate called.

"Coming!" Kirsty yelled, as she and Rachel hurried downstairs.

Kirsty's parents were dressed up as clowns with baggy suits and red noses. They both clapped admiringly when they saw the girls in their costumes.

"You look lovely," said Mrs Tate.

"So do you!" laughed Kirsty.

"Just don't trip over your tails," Mr Tate added as they all set off.

The carnival was in full swing when they arrived. Dusk was falling, and all the stalls were brightly lit. The weather had turned icy cold, but there were still long queues of people waiting for every ride. Rachel and Kirsty were glad that their costumes were cosy.

"It's not going to be easy to spot the goblins in this crowd!" Rachel whispered.

"We'll just have to keep our eyes open," Kirsty replied. "Oh, look, Rachel – hook-a-duck!" She pointed at the stall where little yellow, plastic ducks were bobbing in a tub of water. "Let's have a go."

"We're going to get a cup of tea," said Mrs Tate. "We'll meet you at the fireworks display later, OK, girls?"

Kirsty and Rachel nodded and hurried over to the hook-a-duck stall as Mr and Mrs Tate headed off across the showground.

Kirsty paid the stallholder, and he handed each of the girls a fishing-rod with a hook on the line, so that they could try to catch the ducks.

Rachel concentrated on the duck floating nearest to her. It bobbed away a few times, but at last she managed to catch it. As she pulled it towards her, she heard a tiny voice cry, "Hello, Rachel!"

Rachel was so surprised she almost dropped the duck! Then she looked more closely and saw Kylie perched neatly on the duck's back. Rachel grinned and nudged Kirsty. "I've hooked something better than a duck," she laughed. "Look!"

Quickly the girls put down their fishing-rods and the duck, and moved away from the stall with Kylie.

"Jack Frost is here!" Kylie said breathlessly, fluttering onto Rachel's shoulder. "He thinks his goblins haven't been causing enough mayhem at the carnival, so he's come to keep an eye on them. He's got the Carnival Crown!"

"That's why it's so cold tonight!" exclaimed Kirsty, and Kylie nodded.

"Have you seen any goblins, Kylie?" Rachel asked. But no sooner were the words out of her mouth, than she saw three small figures in jester hats hurrying towards the Tunnel of Love.

"Look!" Rachel gasped, as she spotted their green faces. "Goblins!"

"Well spotted, Rachel," said Kylie.

"Let's follow them," Kirsty suggested.

The three goblins jumped into the front car of the train standing outside the Tunnel of Love. Rachel, Kirsty and Kylie quickly climbed into another carriage a little further back.

The train slowly set off into the tunnel. Inside it was quite dark, so the girls took off their masks and stuffed them in their pockets.

They soon saw that the Tunnel of Love was based around the four seasons.

First they travelled through the spring section, where there were pretty pictures of gardens full of daffodils and bluebells.

Summer came next, and the scenes showed a park with people picnicking and sunbathing. Here the air felt warmer and a park bench stood under a pretty pergola of roses. In the

autumn section it became cooler again, and there were model trees with leaves of red, orange and gold.

The winter scene was the last one and the coldest. Here, there was fake snow on the ground and pictures of people ice-skating and sledging. Models of snowmen and frosty trees were dotted here and there.

The train slowed down as it reached a curve in the track, and the girls were surprised to see the goblins leap off and disappear behind one of the painted scenes.

"Quick!" whispered Rachel. "We'd better follow!"

The girls stepped down from their carriage and hurried to hide behind a plastic tree.

"Hurry up, you idiots!" bellowed a voice from the shadows, making Kylie and the girls jump.

They peeped out from their tree to see Jack Frost sitting on a throne of ice!

"He's wearing the Carnival Crown!" whispered Kirsty excitedly.

Jack Frost glared at his goblins. "You're having too much fun!" he snapped. "You should be spoiling the carnival for the humans, not enjoying it yourselves!"

"Maybe we can creep along behind the scenery, sneak up to the throne and grab the crown right off his head!" Rachel suggested.

"Good idea," Kylie agreed. So Rachel and Kirsty began to edge carefully towards the throne.

"WELL?" Jack Frost roared.

"I've got an idea for ruining the carnival," one goblin volunteered. "We could steal all the toffee-apples and eat them!"

"We can frighten little children!" another shouted.

"And we could put wet paint on the saddles of all the carousel horses!" suggested another goblin eagerly.

"Excellent!" Jack Frost declared, rubbing his hands gleefully. "And I'll keep the Carnival Crown here, so that those pesky fairies can't get their hands on it!"

The goblins cheered. Then, giggling nastily, they all ran back out to the carnival, just as Rachel and Kirsty reached the throne. The girls could see the crown poking above the back of it.

"Can you reach it, Rachel?" Kylie whispered.

"I'll try," Rachel replied, cautiously stretching out her hand. But suddenly the crown was whisked away as Jack Frost leapt to his feet.

The girls jumped, and Kylie almost fell off Rachel's shoulder.

"Thought you could fool me, did you?" Jack Frost sneered, peering round the throne at them. "Well you can't! I knew you were there all the time!"

"We want the crown, please!" Rachel cried.

"Yes, you must give it back!" Kirsty added bravely.

But Jack Frost only laughed, pointed his wand at the girls and fired two ice bolts straight at them.

Ice Lightning

Just in time, Rachel and Kirsty managed to jump out of the way before the lightning bolts struck. When they peeped out again, Jack Frost had jumped into the last car of another train. As it disappeared around the corner, he gave the girls and Kylie a cheery wave.

"After him!" cried Kirsty, and the girls rushed out of the Tunnel of Love.

As soon as they were back in the showground, they realised that the goblins had already started spoiling everything.

"A jester stole my toffee-apple!" sobbed one little boy, while a little girl was complaining that her dress was covered in paint. As Kylie and the girls wondered what to do next, they saw a goblin jester pop out from behind a tree and shout BOO! at a little girl, who burst into tears.

"The goblins are being horrible!" Kirsty said, frowning.

Rachel nodded. "We need to get the Carnival Crown back," she said firmly.

"It won't be easy," Kylie pointed out. "Everyone's in fancy dress, so Jack Frost will be hard to spot."

Suddenly there was a loud BANG.

"Oh!" Rachel exclaimed in surprise.

She glanced up and saw a trail of silver sparks across the sky. "Surely it can't be time for the fireworks yet?" she murmured.

"That's no firework," Kylie cried. "It's one of Jack Frost's ice bolts!"

"It came from over there," Kirsty said, pointing towards the Log Falls ride.

Quickly, the girls dashed towards the ride. Sure enough, there was Jack Frost, and he was using his magic to freeze all the water in the Log Falls waterways.

"Oh, no," Kirsty sighed. "He's found a new way to spoil the carnival!"

Looking very smug, Jack Frost marched off. Rachel, Kylie and Kirsty followed.

"I bet he's looking for another ride to freeze!" said Rachel.

But Jack Frost joined the queue for the Ferris wheel. He stared up at it, his eyes shining.

"He can't freeze that, can he?" Kirsty asked.

"I don't know," Kylie replied, sounding worried. "Let's join the queue behind him. And, girls, put your masks back on so Jack Frost won't recognise you."

Rachel and Kirsty slipped their masks on and joined the queue.

"Just one little ride," Jack Frost was muttering to himself. "I've always wanted to go on a Ferris wheel. And the goblins will never know!" He looked around guiltily, to make sure no goblins were watching. Kirsty and Rachel's hearts pounded as he glanced past them, but he didn't recognise them behind their masks.

"He's going on the Ferris wheel!" Rachel whispered.

"We'll go too!" Kirsty replied.

Looking excited, Jack Frost climbed into a car. Immediately the girls and Kylie jumped into the next one, and the Ferris wheel began to turn.

Rachel glanced upwards. Jack Frost's car was above theirs as they were lifted into the air. But Rachel realised that once they got past the highest point and started to move back down, Jack Frost would be below them. *If only we had something to hook the crown with*, Rachel thought, *we could lift it straight off Jack Frost's head!*

Suddenly, Rachel spotted the hook-a-duck stall. "I've got an idea!" she exclaimed. "Kylie, could you magic a fishing-rod with a big hook at the end of the line – like the ones for hook-a-duck?"

"Oh!" Kirsty looked excited. "You mean, we can hook-a-crown!"

"No problem," Kylie laughed.

She fluttered into the air and waved her wand. With a flash of sparkles, a shiny gold fishing-rod appeared in Rachel's hands.

"We're going over the top of the wheel," Kirsty announced. "Now we're above Jack Frost."

Rachel took off her mask and leant forwards, trying to catch the Carnival Crown below her with the hook on the end of her fishing line. She came close, but the wind kept blowing the hook the wrong way. Kylie fluttered down, gently caught the hook and attached it to the crown.

Hardly daring to breathe, Rachel began to lift the crown off Jack Frost's head…

A Queen is Crowned

Jack Frost didn't notice a thing as Rachel drew the crown upwards. He was having too much fun enjoying the ride!

"Well done, Rachel," Kirsty whispered as she freed the crown from the fishing line.

Kylie beamed at the girls. "Now we can make sure the carnival ends happily," she said. "We'll be just in time for the crowning ceremony!"

All the rides were coming to a halt now. The parade had started and soon it would be time for the Carnival King or Queen to be crowned. As soon as the Ferris wheel stopped, the girls jumped out of their car. Rachel glanced nervously at Jack Frost, but he still hadn't noticed that the crown had gone.

Just then a goblin hurried up to him. "The crown!" he shouted, pointing at Jack Frost's head. "Where's it gone?"

Jack Frost clapped his hands to his head and immediately realised that the crown wasn't there. Furiously he spun round and his icy glare met Rachel's. Her heart sinking, Rachel remembered that she hadn't put her mask back on.

"You again!" Jack Frost shouted. Then he spotted the crown in Kirsty's hands. "I want that crown!"

"Run!" shouted Kylie.

The girls took to their heels, Kylie clinging to Kirsty's shoulder. They headed for the main stage, where the crowning ceremony was due to take place. Jack Frost raced after them.

"The Carnival Master's on stage," Rachel panted. "We're almost there!"

But at the same time, the girls could hear Jack Frost chanting a spell behind them. "Don't think you can escape from me. These balls will stop you, wait and see!" he cried.

As the girls passed the coconut shy, a bucket of balls overturned and the balls rolled and bounced across the grass, right under the girls' feet. Rachel slipped and Kirsty stumbled. The crown flew out of Kirsty's hands and sailed through the air towards the stage.

"Oh, no!" Rachel cried as she saw Jack Frost racing after it.

Jack Frost caught the crown at the edge of the stage, just as the Carnival Master stepped up to make an announcement.

"I'm afraid the Carnival Crown has gone missing," he said sadly.

"But the Carnival King or Queen will still

receive free tickets to next year's carnival."

But as the Carnival Master spoke, a spotlight came on and lit up Jack Frost in a blaze of white light. He stood there, blinking, crown in hand.

"The Carnival Crown!" gasped the Carnival Master, hurrying over to Jack Frost. "You've found it! That's wonderful!" The crowd applauded wildly as the Carnival Master shook Jack Frost warmly by the hand.

"And what a fantastic costume!" he added admiringly.

Rachel, Kirsty and Kylie watched as Jack Frost was drawn on stage by the Carnival Master in a storm of applause.

"Look, Jack Frost is blushing!" Kylie whispered.

And it was true! Jack Frost was clearly enjoying all the attention. He had a very smug look on his face.

"Please help me announce the winner," said the Carnival Master, and Jack Frost looked even more pleased.

Rachel nudged Kirsty as she noticed the goblins cheering at the front of the crowd.

The Carnival Master held up a piece of paper, and Jack Frost read out:

"Our Carnival Queen this year is Alexandra Kirby, for her beautiful princess costume!"

A little blonde girl in a pretty princess outfit walked on stage smiling. The Carnival Master helped her to sit on the golden throne and then turned to Jack Frost for the crown.

Jack Frost frowned, and clung to the crown as the Carnival Master tried to take it. But, eventually, he had to let go. He couldn't do anything else in front of such a large audience.

As the Carnival Queen was crowned, he stomped sulkily off stage. But immediately a crowd of children surrounded him.

"Please can I have your autograph?" asked one little boy.

"How did you find the crown?" asked another.

"Can we take your photo?" begged two little girls.

Looking flustered, Jack Frost tried to move away, but the children followed.

"Jack Frost has a fan club!" Kylie remarked, laughing, as she and the girls headed away from the stage. "Girls, how can I ever thank you? Now Sunnydays Carnival can move on for other children to enjoy."

"We were glad to help!" Rachel smiled.

"And it must be nearly time for the fireworks," added Kirsty. "We'd better go and find Mum and Dad."

As she spoke, a huge, glittering cloud of fairy dust exploded in the air ahead of them.

"Look, Kirsty!" Rachel gasped, as the dust began to clear. In front of them the carousel was spinning and sparkling with fairy magic. And there, on a painted unicorn's back, sat King Oberon and Queen Titania.

Very Special Guests

"What are you doing here?" Rachel asked, looking delighted as the King and Queen flew over to her.

"We've only ever seen you in Fairyland before," said Kirsty.

King Oberon smiled. "We've come to thank you for all your help," he said.

"Thanks to you, Sunnydays Carnival is saved!" added the Queen.

"What about Jack Frost?" Kirsty asked.

"Don't worry about him!" the King said, pointing at Jack Frost, who was happily signing autographs for all the children. "He's enjoying himself."

"Jack Frost loves to be the centre of attention," the Queen explained. "While he's so popular, he won't cause any trouble for Sunnydays."

"Come here!" Jack Frost was telling his goblins. "Collect up these autograph books and carnival programmes. I'll sign them all!"

Rachel and Kirsty laughed.

"So the carnival's safe at last!" said Rachel.

"Yes, and these are to say thank you," Queen Titania replied. She lifted her wand and touched first Kirsty's hand, then Rachel's. Suddenly each girl found herself holding a tiny, glittering model of a carousel!

"Look, Rachel," Kirsty gasped in delight. "They're exactly the same as the Sunnydays carousel!"

"And the horses move round too!" Rachel added, turning her carousel. "They're beautiful!"

A whooshing noise made them all look up, just in time to see a shower of red and green sparks light up the sky.

"The fireworks display is starting," said King Oberon. "You'd better hurry back to Kirsty's parents, girls. Kylie, the Queen and I have work to do!"

The Queen smiled and winked at Rachel and Kirsty. "We have to make sure the fireworks are extra-special this year!" she laughed. And Kylie clapped her hands in joy.

"Goodbye!" cried Rachel and Kirsty. "And thank you for our beautiful gifts."

The fairies waved their wands, and then zoomed into the night sky in a shower of rainbow-coloured sparkles. Seconds later, as the girls joined Kirsty's parents, the sky was filled

with a mass of fireworks glittering in all the colours of the rainbow.

"Goodness me!" gasped the Carnival Master, looking surprised. "I don't remember buying such fabulous fireworks!"

Rachel and Kirsty grinned at each other. They were the only ones who knew that there was a little royal fairy magic adding a lot of extra sparkle to the Sunnydays Carnival.

Here's Kylie the Carnival Fairy!

Kylie and the girls managed to stop mean Jack Frost from causing trouble the Sunnydays Carnival!

Happiest hobby

Riding on rollercoasters and enjoying the view from the top of the Ferris wheel!

Personality

Fun-loving, friendly and loyal.

All the other fairies know that Kylie is incredibly kind, generous, and lots of fun!

Fairy playmates

The Dance Fairies and the Fun Day Fairies.

I make sure that carnivals are fabulous and fun for everyone!
Favourite colour
I love all colours - the brighter the better! My particular favourites are yellow and red.
Yummiest food
Popcorn and toffee apples!
Fairy outfit
Kylie's gorgeous multi-coloured skirt is made from lots of pretty ribbons. Her bracelets and hair accessories are also created from different lengths of silky fabric.

Meet Jack Frost and the Goblins

Jack Frost has an army of naughty goblins to help him create chaos. Whenever there's a chill in the air, the fairies must be on their guard...

I will have my revenge for not being invited to the Fairyland Midsummer Ball!

Favourite colour
Ice-white.

Name
Jack Frost.

Personality
Cold-hearted, jealous and mean.

Home
His turreted frozen Ice Castle.

Frosty friends
Only his band of grumpy goblin servants.

Most trusted magic
His powerful banishment spell.

Frosty features
A chill breeze always swirls around Jack's bony figure and angry face. His ice-blue robes are trimmed with sharp icicles. Frost glints in his white hair and beard. His pointy elf boots leave icy footprints behind him.

Horrible hobby
Jack thinks he's a magnificent artist. He's always etching frozen designs on window panes, but the fact that no one ever seems to notice them never fails to put him in a frosty mood.

Name
The Goblins.

Personality
Selfish, sneaky but very dim.

Home
The dungeons of Jack Frost's Ice Castle.

Favourite food
Goblins are so greedy they'll eat anything, even dog food!

Horrible hobby
Taking fairy possessions and trampling on flowers.

Frosty friends
None. Most goblins even fight amongst themselves.

Worst time of year
Unfortunately it's winter. Jack Frost gives them lots of jobs to do and goblins hate having cold feet!

Frosty features
The tallest goblins are as high as Kirsty and Rachel's waists, but Jack Frost often uses his powers to make them taller or smaller! All goblins are ugly green creatures with big feet and sharp, pointy ears and noses.

The Rainbow Fairies

Meet all the Rainbow Magic fairies in these exciting storybooks!

978-1-84362-0167

978-1-84362-0174

978-1-84362-0181

978-1-84362-0198

978-1-84362-0204

978-1-84362-0211

978-1-84362-0228

The Weather Fairies

978-1-84362-6336

978-1-84362-6343

978-1-84362-6350

978-1-84362-6411

978-1-84362-6367

978-1-84362-6374

978-1-84362-6381

The Party Fairies

978-1-84362-8187

978-1-84362-8194

978-1-84362-8200

978-1-84362-8217

978-1-84362-8224

978-1-84362-8231

978-1-84362-8248

The Jewel Fairies

978-1-84362-9580

978-1-84362-9542

978-1-84362-9559

978-1-84362-9566

978-1-84362-9573

978-1-84362-9535

978-1-84362-9597

The Pet Keeper Fairies

978-1-84616-1667

978-1-84616-1704

978-1-84616-1681

978-1-84616-1698

978-1-84616-1674

978-1-84616-1728

978-1-84616-1711

The Fun Day Fairies

978-1-84616-1889

978-1-84616-1896

978-1-84616-1902

978-1-84616-1919

978-1-84616-1926

978-1-84616-1933

978-1-84616-1940

The Petal Fairies

978-1-84616-4576

978-1-84616-4583

978-1-84616-4590

978-1-84616-4606

978-1-84616-4620

978-1-84616-4613

978-1-84616-4644

The Dance Fairies

978-1-84616-4903

978-1-84616-4910

978-1-84616-4927

978-1-84616-4934

978-1-84616-4958

978-1-84616-4965

978-1-84616-4972

The Sporty Fairies

978-1-84616-8888

978-1-84616-8895

978-1-84616-8901

978-1-84616-8918

978-1-84616-8925

978-1-84616-8932

978-1-84616-8949

The Music Fairies

978-1-40830-0336

978-1-40830-0305

978-1-40830-0299

978-1-40830-0282

978-1-40830-0312

978-1-40830-0275

978-1-40830-0329

The Magical Animal Fairies

978-1-40830-3498

978-1-40830-3559

978-1-40830-3511

978-1-40830-3504

978-1-40830-3542

978-1-40830-3528

978-1-40830-3535

Look out for the Green Fairies in September

Specials

Holly the Christmas Fairy: 978-1-84362-6619
Summer the Holiday Fairy: 978-1-84362-9603
Stella the Star Fairy: 978-1-84362-8699
Kylie the Carnival Fairy: 978-1-84616-1759
Paige the Pantomime Fairy: 978-1-84616-2091
Flora the Fancy Dress Fairy: 978-1-84616-5054
Chrissie the Wish Fairy: 978-1-84616-5061
Shannon the Ocean Fairy: 978-1-40830-025-1
Gabriella the Snow Kingdom Fairy: 978-1-40830-034-3

978-1-40830-348-1

All priced at £3.99. The Specials are priced at £5.99.
Rainbow Magic books are available from all good bookshops, or can be ordered direct from the publisher: Orchard Books, PO BOX 29, Douglas IM99 1BQ.
Credit card orders please telephone 01624 836000 or fax 01624 837033 or visit our website: www.orchardbooks.co.uk or e-mail: bookshop@enterprise.net for details.

To order please quote title, author and ISBN and your full name and address. Cheques and postal orders should be made payable to 'Bookpost plc.'
Postage and packing is FREE within the UK (overseas customers should add £2.00 per book).
Prices and availability are subject to change.

Farewell, Fairy Friends